MW01349229

Chase God & Chase Adventure!
Holly Rehberg

This book is dedicated to Emslee and Piper. May you always follow your dreams no matter when you start. Just start. --- Love, Mom. Thank you too, to my husband Randall for his continued support through this process.

This book is also dedicated, in loving memory, to Jennifer Lynne Trent, a friend, teaching colleague, and impassioned reading teacher. Jennifer beat cancer in January 2021, only to lose her life to the corona virus a few weeks later. Support Jennifer's love for teaching struggling readers by donating this book to your local schools, libraries, or donate in Jennifer's name to your favorite charity.

Cal the Camel and His Kayaking Adventure

Copyright © 2021 by Holly Rehberg All rights reserved.

All images, logos, quotes, and trademarks included in this book are subject to use according to trademark and copyright laws of the United States of America.

No part of this book may be distributed, posted, or reproduced in any form by digital or mechanical means without prior written permission of the publisher, except in the case of brief quotations embodied in critical articles and reviews. For permissions, more information, or to book an event contact the author here: www.calthecamel.com.

ISBN 978-1-7366580-0-0

Library of Congress Control Number: 2021902761

Published by Holly Rehberg. Broken Arrow, Oklahoma

First Edition. 2021. Printed in Canada by Friesens Corporation

by Holly Rehberg

Cal the Camel was a VERY curious camel who longed for adventure. He lived in a wilderness park and wished that just ONCE, he too could go on an adventure.

The wilderness park attracted visitors from all over the nation, traveling on their own adventures.

The visitors would
drive through the park
hoping to catch a glimpse
of various wild animals including... camels.

Cal and his friends would entertain the
visitors by looking cute and getting up
close to lick their windows.

The visitors would squeal in delight.

Even though licking windows, and seeing new visitors was fun, Cal longed for at least ONE exciting adventure before his next birthday.

Feeling like it might never happen, Cal decided to go to bed early.

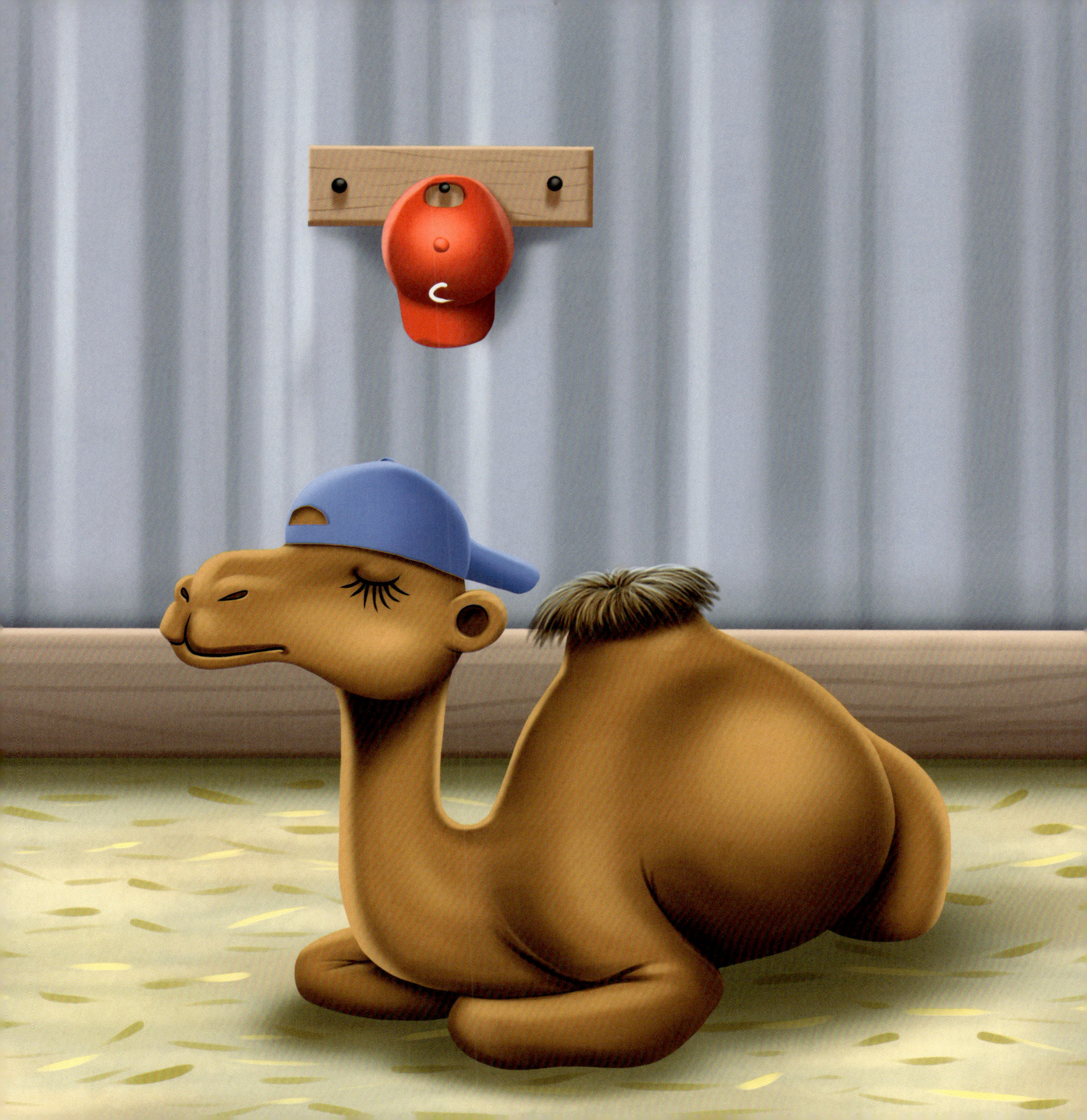

The next morning, Cal woke up a little upset.
He figured today would be just like any other day.

B-O-R-I-N-G... Boring.

But....as he heard the crackle of gravel, a car approached. Looking up quickly, Cal was ENTHRALLED!

This car looked different than most—two, long, funny-looking shoes sat on the roof. As Cal watched, his caretaker Jim asked the visitors about the objects on top of their car. It turned out that they were not shoes at all—they were kayaks.

The family had traveled a great distance to kayak on the nearby lake and were now headed to a large waterfall.

Wait ....just.... a.... minute! Did they say KAYAKS???

KAYAKS were the most glorious things he had ever seen, and Cal knew immediately that today was going to be different. That TODAY he was going on an adventure.

C

Cal's imagination ran wild as he thought up a scheme to get inside those kayaks.

He followed the car past his zebra and giraffe friends and yelled to his mother that he would be back later. She yelled back, "Take your little sister and be back by dark."

His sister trotted up behind him with questions.

Cal told her to be quiet and to follow along if she was interested in an adventure.

While the family stopped to get out and take pictures of the new baby giraffe, Cal and Callie managed to climb into the kayaks. The family finished their pictures and headed for the falls.

Cal was SOOO excited.
His ADVENTURE was about to begin.

Once at the falls, the family climbed out of the car to go swimming, and after the coast was clear, Cal and his sister carried the kayaks on their humps, up to the falls.

When they reached the pool at the top, Cal secured their protective gear just before they launched into the water.

They had fun spinning in circles, going backwards, and splashing each other with their paddles.

They were having so much fun they didn't
realize they were inching closer to the edge.

As they inched closer and closer to the waterfall, there was no time to paddle backwards AND no time to prepare.
There was only one thing left to do. **SCREAM!!!!!**

Cal and Callie screamed all the way down the huge waterfall. Cal took a second to take in his surroundings and realized he was right in the middle of HIS ADVENTURE!

Once they hit the pool below, Cal made sure Callie was ok and helped pull her to the bank to get out.

Giggling and talking about their adventure, they secured the kayaks on their backs and raced to the parking lot.

They knew time was running out—they had to get home before dark.

As it sunk in that they hadn't thought of a plan to get home, Callie started crying. How WERE they going to get home?

Excited to see the family coming back to their car, Cal and Callie noticed the youngest family member was crying. She had forgotten her favorite kitty at the wilderness park.

Both camels were relieved.
They were going home.

Back in the park, the family stopped at the main office to retrieve their stuffed kitty. Cal and his sister hopped out of the kayaks and trotted home just in time for dinner.

As Cal's family began to eat, his mom asked what they had been up to all day.

Before Callie could give it away, smiling, Cal replied, "Oh, you know, nothing major, just the same old boring stuff."

Their mom gave them both a funny look but didn't question any further.

After dinner, Cal went to see his friends and tell them about his adventure. He could hear the faint sound of gravel crackling as the family left the park, chattering to each other, that today had been one of their most favorite adventures EVER.

Thinking about his day, with a smile on his face,
Cal could not have agreed more.

Tiny Hope Clouds

As you read through Cal's adventure, did you notice a tiny cloud on almost every page? There is a Bible story in 1 Kings 18: 43-46 that tells how the people of Samaria had not seen rain for three years. This devastated their land, crops and cattle. A man named Elijah prayed and prayed for God to make it rain. Elijah sent a friend to go and look for any sign of rain out over the sea. His friend did not see one. After praying some more, Elijah sent his friend back to look again. Excitedly his friend was happy to report that he saw a cloud the size of a man's hand developing over the sea. This gave Elijah hope that much rain was soon to come. As you go through your life, look for tiny clouds of hope that symbolize God's love for you.

About the Author

Holly Rehberg resides in Oklahoma with her family. She is a special education teacher by trade and has always wanted to author a book. She loves to travel and like Cal loves a good adventure.

About Cal the Camel

Cal the Camel also resides in Oklahoma with his family. He enjoys the outdoors, wearing hats, and going on adventures.

You can find him here: www.calthecamel.com

Thank you to Atlin and Avery from Vancouver, BC Canada for inspiring Cal's kayak and safety gear.

An extra thank you goes to:
Jodelle, Beth, Norma, Jennifer, Krista, Brandon, and Julie for your collaboration efforts. Also to Authorpreneur Central for their continued patience and guidance in making my idea a reality.